Indian Landing School Library
Penfield Central District

Penfield Indian Landing

PEIL32594

W9-AAE-044

E
KUS

PEIL32594

Kusugak, Michael
Northern lights: the
soccer trails

$17.00

Michael Arvaarluk Kusugak

NORTHERN LIGHTS
THE SOCCER TRAILS

Art: Vladyana Krykorka

ᐊᖅᓴᓕᓵᑦ ᐃᓄᕕᐱᓃᒡᒎᖅ ᐊᖅᓴᖅᑐᑦ

ANNICK PRESS LTD.
Toronto • New York • Vancouver

A **Teacher's Guide** is available that offers a program of classroom study based on this book. It is available for free at www.annickpress.com and click on "For Teachers".

©1993 Michael Arvaarluk Kusugak (text)
©1993 Vladyana Krykorka (illustrations)
Designed by Vladyana Krykorka.

Seventh printing, January 2003

Annick Press Ltd.

All rights reserved. No part of this work covered by the copyrights hereon
may be reproduced or used in any form or by any means – graphic, electronic,
or mechanical – without the prior written permission of the publisher.

We acknowledge the support of the Canada Council for the Arts, the Ontario
Arts Council, and the Government of Canada through the Book Publishing
Industry Development Program (BPIDP) for our publishing activities.

The publisher wishes to thank Rhoda Karetak, of Rankin Inlet,
N.W.T., for permission to photograph her amaut (decorative parka).

Cataloging in Publication Data
    Kusugak, Michael
        Northern lights : the soccer trails
    ISBN 1-55037-339-0 (bound) ISBN 1-55037-338-2 (pbk.)

    1. Inuit - Canada - Juvenile fiction.* I. Krykorka.
    Vladyana. II. Title.

    PS8571.U78N6 1993   jC813'.54   C93-094134-9
    PZ7.K98No 1993

Distributed in Canada by:
Firefly Books Ltd.
3680 Victoria Park Avenue
Willowdale, ON
M2H 3K1

Published in the U.S.A. by Annick Press (U.S.) Ltd.
Distributed in the U.S.A. by:
Firefly Books (U.S.) Inc.
P.O. Box 1338
Ellicott Station
Buffalo, NY 14205

Printed and bound in Canada by Friesens, Altona, Manitoba.

www.annickpress.com

to my father, Kusugak, who showed me hope
to my uncle, Kreelak, who brought the stories to life
to Jack Hildes who showed me undying friendship
to my uncle, Ussak, who taught me patience and
to my Anaanattialluaq (The-Perfect-Grandmother-For-Me),
  Tartak, who showed me love.
I see them when the northern lights are out.
  and
to Naanasee, just the thought of whom makes me happy.

M.A.K.

To my father, who in his youth was a champion soccer player.

V.K.

A long time ago, when Kataujaq was little, her mother said, "We called you Kataujaq because, when you were born, you were as pretty as a rainbow." She put her nose to Kataujaq's, sniffed and said "Mamaq," which means "You smell so nice." You see, that is the way we kiss. Some people call it rubbing noses but it is really sniffing. And Kataujaq hugged her mother by her neck, pressed her nose on her face and said "Mamaq!" Kataujaq just loved her mother.

In spring, the sun was still up in the sky when Kataujaq went to bed. When she woke up, early the next morning, it was already way up in the sky again. In spring, they would all go fishing.

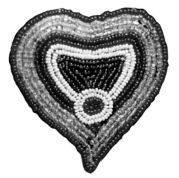

They travelled on the sea ice. Kataujaq sat with her mother and her grandmother in the big canoe on the sled. It was very rough and there was a lot of water on the ice. The dogs' paws went "Slosh, slosh, slosh, slosh..." and the sled creaked. Kataujaq's father ran along beside it, holding onto the bow of the canoe, pushing this way, pulling that way, guiding the sled. "Hut, hut, hut," he said to the dogs, and they turned left.

Sometimes they had to go over big cracks in the ice. Kataujaq's father threw the dogs into the water and made them swim across. As they climbed out of the water, the dogs shook their fur, throwing tiny droplets of water everywhere which sparkled in the bright sunlight. Then Kataujaq's father made the dogs pull the sled across with the canoe and the people in it. Kataujaq and her mother screamed, "Aaiee!!" and hugged each other really hard because the water was dark and ominous looking. And sometimes they came upon seal holes where the water was flowing in, swirling like a whirlpool. Just the thought of them made Kataujaq shudder. She was glad she had her mother to hang on to.

When they got back on land they went to a lake called The Nose. It has a string of little islands in it that look like noses sticking up out of the ice. Kataujaq's mother caught a fish that was as big as Kataujaq.

In summer, Kataujaq loved to go for walks. One day, as she walked, Kataujaq picked a flower. It was a teeny tiny flower with delicate white petals. "My Mom will like this," she said to herself. She collected many more beautiful tiny flowers. When she got home, she gave them to her mother. Her mother hugged her and kissed her and said, "They are beautiful. Thank you." She put them in a glass and kept them for a long time. She kept them even when they were dried up and did not look very nice anymore. Then Kataujaq went for another walk and collected more tiny flowers.

Sometimes she collected nice rocks: grey ones, white caribou-fat ones, flat ones and smooth round ones. And her mother loved every one. She put them on the window sill. One day, Kataujaq's father tried to throw one away. Her mother said, "What are you doing? Put it back!" She was very stern about it and he put it back.

Late summer, just after the weather turns cool and the mosquitoes have gone, is the very best time to pick berries. The ground turns a fuzzy brown colour, it begins to get dark at night and the geese begin to form flocks, getting ready to fly away before winter comes. It was Kataujaq's *most* favourite time of year because she got to spend so much time outside with her mother. They picked berries on the long esker that lay just north of their house. Kataujaq's mother loved to pick berries. It took them a long time to fill a big can, but they did it. Kataujaq's face and hands turned purple with berry juice because she ate most of the berries she picked. Oh, what fun it was.

Sometimes they just played together. Kataujaq's mother would juggle stones and sing a juggling song:

> **Ai jaa ju ru jun nii**
> **A ja jaa ju ru jun nii**
> **Three for my cousin**
> **One for me**
> **Sounds like thunder**
> **Sounds like thunder**
> **Rainbow in the sky**
> **Rainbow in the sky**

Her mother taught Kataujaq all kinds of wonderful things that they had done when she herself was little. They had so much fun.

But that was a long time ago.

One day, a big sickness came. So many people were sick. Kataujaq's mother coughed and coughed and they sent her away, way down south in an aeroplane. And she never came home again. Nobody told Kataujaq what had happened. She was too little. Her mother just never came home again.

It was such a long time ago. Now Kataujaq was a big girl; well, almost a big girl. But she still missed her mother a lot. These days she picked tiny flowers for her kindly grandmother, but it was not the same. When she picked berries on the long esker, just north of her house, she thought about her mother. When she picked up a nice rock, she thought about her mother. Sometimes, when she was alone, Kataujaq cried. Sometimes, when she went to bed at night and thoughts came, she cried a lot.

In the fall, ice forms on the lakes and the sea. At night, when the sky is clear, you can see the stars, millions of them, twinkling through the moonlight. And sometimes you can see the droppings of the stars come streaking across the sky and disappear before they reach the horizon. Kataujaq loved to watch the sky and the stars. Sometimes she would wait a long time to see star droppings streak across the sky.

It was in early winter that the people in her village liked to go out and play soccer. They made a soccer ball out of caribou skin and stuffed it full of dry moss and fur. Then at night, in the moonlight, they went out on the sea ice, set up two goals made of ice blocks and played. Anybody who came down to the sea-ice joined in the game. They would run for miles and miles, all night long. It was such fun.

Sometimes the northern lights came out.
They are thin strands of light, thousands of thin strands of light,
that move about from here to there like thousands of people running
around, following one another.

Kataujaq's grandmother liked to come out and watch the people play soccer too, and one night, when Kataujaq was feeling very sad and lonely, her grandmother told her a story.

"People die," she said. "And, when they die, their souls leave their bodies and go up into the heavens, and there they live. The thousands of people who have passed before us all live up there in the sky. When they were on earth, they too liked to play soccer. And, even though they no longer live among us, they still like to play. So, on a clear moonlit night, they go out on the giant field up there and play soccer. You can see them, thousands of them, all running around chasing their soccer ball all over the sky."

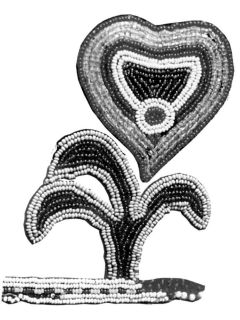

Kataujaq watched the northern lights. The thousands of strands of light looked like they were all running around after each other chasing a soccer ball. Kataujaq's grandmother continued her story:

"But, unlike us, they are immortal now and nothing hurts them anymore, so they use a huge, frozen walrus head with big tusks for a soccer ball. When they give that walrus head a mighty kick, it flies across the sky, and they all chase it from one corner of the sky to the other. If you whistle they will come closer, and, if you keep whistling, they will come even closer. But beware, they may come too near. If they do, that walrus head might come swooping down and, 'Bonk!' knock your head off. When they come too close, rub your fingernails together so they make a clicking sound. That will make them go away."

Kataujaq whistled. The northern lights came closer. She whistled some more and they came closer and still closer. She thought she heard a cracking sound. Was it the sound of a mighty kick on a hard, frozen walrus head? And she thought she heard a "Whoosh!" as it came whizzing by. It was an eerie sound, like giant tusks slicing the air. It sounded awfully near. Quickly, she rubbed her fingernails together, making a clicking sound, and eventually the northern lights began to go farther away.

"Is my mother up there?" Kataujaq asked her grandmother.

"Of course she is," her grandmother replied. "When it is like this I, too, like to come out here. I come to see your grandfather. He was a kind man who loved to play soccer. He would have loved you. He always wanted a grand-daughter. Now he is up there with all the other people who have passed away. Seeing him having a wonderful time makes me feel so much better."

Kataujaq watched the northern lights play their game for a long time. She thought she could see her mother running around with all of them up there. She seemed to be having a good time. As her mother turned to run, Kataujaq thought she saw her smile down. Kataujaq was glad her mother had not gone away at all. She was not so lonely anymore. It made her feel so much better.

Sometime, when the moon is out and the stars are twinkling brightly in the frosty air, you should go outside and take a look. Maybe you will see the northern lights way up in the sky. They really are the souls of people who have died and, like us, they like to go out and have a good time. They love to play soccer. And if you look closely, maybe you will see someone special whom you thought had gone away forever. That special person has not really gone away at all. It is the most wonderful thing.   Taima